The Wonders of Donal O'Donnell

The Wonders of Donal O'Donnell

A FOLKTALE OF IRELAND

GARY SCHMIDT

Illustrated by LOREN LONG

Henry Holt and Company
New York

For Brian Christopher Roseberry,
and for those who love him
—G. S.

To Griff, thank you
—L. L.

Henry Holt and Company, LLC, *Publishers since 1866*
115 West 18th Street, New York, New York 10011
www.henryholt.com

Library of Congress Cataloging-in-Publication Data
Schmidt, Gary D.
The wonders of Donal O'Donnell: a folktale of Ireland /
by Gary Schmidt; illustrated by Loren Long.
Summary: The stories of three peddlers are told to Donal O'Donnell and his wife
one stormy night and begin to heal their hearts, broken by the death of their son.
[1. Folklore—Ireland.] I. Long, Loren, ill. II. Title.
PZ8.1.S3513 Wo 2002   398.2'09417'02—dc21   00-47301

ISBN 0-8050-6516-4
First Edition—2002 / Designed by David Caplan
Printed in the United States of America on acid-free paper. ∞
1   3   5   7   9   10   8   6   4   2
The artist used acrylic on canvas to create the illustrations for this book.

Contents

***

Donal O'Donnell, Sorcha, and Their Boyo

‿⟲⟳‿

D onal O'Donnell was a heart-scalded man. He and Sorcha lived alone on the mountainside of Slieve Bernagh, high above the village of Killaloe. They remembered a time when their door was always open and their boyo carried the laughing sunlight in and out on his shoulders. The grass was greener where he walked, the air brighter, the water colder. The stories they told together as they tended the puck goats! The music they played together to lighten their hearts and feet!

But the day came when their boyo lay still, stiller, and then still forever. And the grass was no longer green, the air no longer bright, the sunlight no longer laughing. Their boyo was gone to the dim world, and his dying closed their hearts and their door.

Now when Donal O'Donnell shushed the puck goats out of their pen in the morning, he would call, "It's late

that I'll be back. Bar the door and bolt it, for I'll have no one in my house this day."

"Which is what I do every morning, Donal O'Donnell," Sorcha would reply sorrowfully.

And Donal O'Donnell would drive his puck goats up Slieve Bernagh. A lonesome walk Donal O'Donnell took along the path he had once taken so lightly with his boyo. A lonesome walk it was without his skipping steps, without the hawthorn-berry dark of his eyes. Without him.

♦　♦　♦

WINTER CAME TOO EARLY that year. One afternoon, black clouds scuttled over Slieve Bernagh, a cold sleet pelting out of them. On the heights, Donal O'Donnell beat his arms against his sides and huddled the puck goats closer. The wind wrestled itself down under his collar and frosted him no matter which way he faced.

Down by the farmhouse, Sorcha heard the sleet spatter against the windows. Then, such a pounding that it might have been the giant Finn M'Coul, his very self, knuckling at the door. Sorcha grasped the shawl

9

around her shoulders. "Who knocks?" she called.

"A storm-stayed peddler."

"It's not here that you'll be finding a place."

"You'll not be turning away a man in a cold like this!"

Sorcha hesitated, then quickly lifted the bar, drew the bolt, and opened the door. The wind pushed in a frozen peddler, his pack lashed by icy ropes to his back. "The dark," he gasped, "has the banshees in it."

Sorcha barred and bolted the door, then led the peddler to the hearth. And when he sat, a wonder! The wind howling down the chimney quieted, and the fire brightened. "The blessing on you," he whispered through chattering lips.

"You'll only be staying until my Donal comes."

"I'll hold by the fire till then, and afterwards, God protect all souls out on Slieve Bernagh tonight."

"Amen to that," said Sorcha, and put a teakettle on to boil.

The smell of brewing herbs had filled the room when another knocking sent Sorcha to unbarring and unbolting the door. It would be Donal O'Donnell, she knew. And how was it she would explain the peddler? But when she drew it open and shouldered the door against the shove of the wind, it was not Donal O'Donnell who came in but another peddler, as frozen as the first.

"A blessing on all in this house," he cried, "and if a night's lodging is to be found here, a blessing again."

Sorcha barred and bolted the door, then led him quickly to the fire. She pressed his hands around a warm mug of tea and set him by the crackling blaze. "The Dear hold you close for opening your door," said the second peddler.

"As for that," said Sorcha, "it's not here that you'll be getting a night's lodging. Warm your bones, but you both must be gone before my Donal returns."

And then, once more, a knocking, a desperate knocking. Sorcha rushed to the door, unbarred and unbolted it, and another peddler, white with the sleet, fell into the light of the room.

Sorcha and the two peddlers carried him to the fire.

They chafed his arms and legs, poured scalding tea down his throat, and wrapped him in blankets. The fire snapped joyfully now and danced its rosy glow across them all the while. "It's to heaven I am," said the third peddler.

"Not to heaven," said Sorcha. "To the home of my Donal."

"Then the Lord's blessing on this house," said the peddler. "The Dear's blessing forever and ever."

Suddenly the door banged open, for Sorcha had forgotten to bar and bolt it. There stood Donal O'Donnell on the threshold. Ice layered his shoulders, and his face was white with his own frozen breath. He stared at the three peddlers sitting at his hearth, at the fire where he and his boyo had sipped hot tea from their mugs after coming down the mountainside.

"Then this is how you remember to bar and bolt the door, woman," said Donal O'Donnell, thunder in his voice.

"My dear," said Sorcha, brushing the ice off Donal O'Donnell's coat, "what would you have me do on such a night, for all love?"

"Do!" he cried. "Do!" But suddenly the fire crackled in just such a way, and the scent of the peat came up just so, that he could almost see his boyo sitting there, warming his hands, and Sorcha setting a shawl around his shoulders. He could almost hear him call, "Da, come sit by me. Here, by the fire." Sure, he could almost hear his boyo.

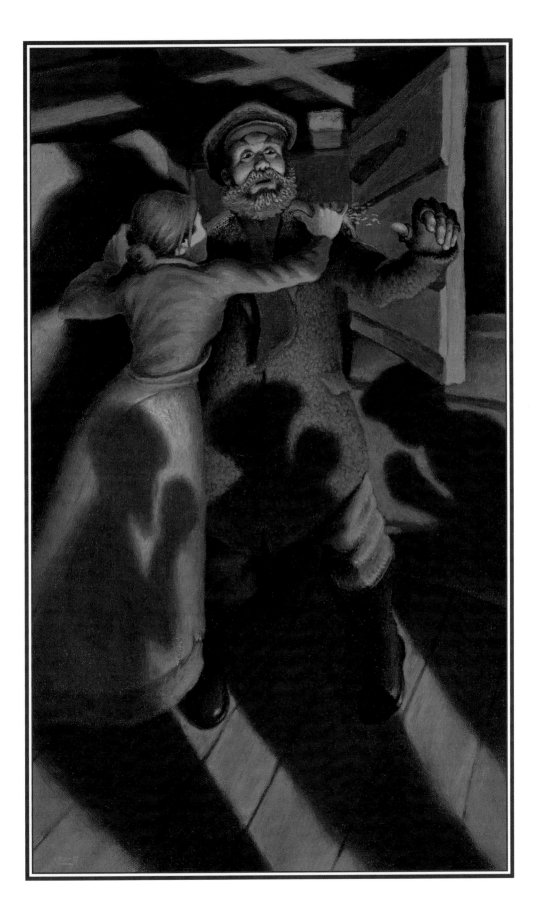

Donal O'Donnell shook his head. "Faith, I would not have left the puck goats out on a night like this. You could do no less."

He hung his coat on a peg by the door and laid his hand on the small cloak carefully kept beside it. Then he crossed to the hearth.

"Fill your pipes and we'll share a smoke," he told the peddlers, holding out his tobacco pouch. "And when we're done, I'll guide you the way to Killaloe."

They thanked him, and after Donal O'Donnell lit

their pipes with an ember they settled back, puffing the sweet smoke to a cloud around them, their feet stretched to the blaze.

"Your name," said the first peddler in the long quiet, "is Donal, is it?"

Donal O'Donnell nodded, watching the embers.

"So is it mine, too," the first peddler said. "Donal O'Sheary by name."

"Is it now?" said Donal O'Donnell quietly, as if he hardly heard.

"God's own truth, but mine is Donal as well," said the second peddler. "Donal O'Neary by name."

"Three Donals under one roof," marveled Sorcha, stoking the peat.

"But there are four," laughed the third peddler, taking his pipe from his mouth and bowing his head to them. "Donal O'Leary by name."

"Faith, a wonder," said Donal O'Donnell. "But my pipe is almost finished, and you'll be wanting to be on your way." Donal O'Donnell leaned over and knocked his ashes on the hearth.

"If it's wonders you'll be after," said Donal O'Sheary, "it won't be far that you'll have to go. I've a wonder that turns four Donals at one fire as plain as a bog pine, if you'll hear my story."

Now Donal O'Donnell dearly loved a story, and not since his boyo lay down had one been told by this hearth. He glanced at Sorcha, and she smiled the faintest smile across her lips. Donal O'Donnell filled his pipe again, and since he could do no less, he passed his tobacco pouch around to the three peddlers. "Well and good," said Donal O'Donnell. "Say on."

And so Donal O'Sheary did, and he told this tale.

The Tale of Donal O'Sheary

◆ THE FIRST PEDDLER ◆

One year, my father and I gathered five hundred stooks of oats and barley against the winter snows. Five hundred stooks as high as two men, as broad as four. But one morning, what should I find when I went out but a stook missing, gone as if it had never been. The next morning, another gone, and not a sight nor sign of it. Another on the next, and another on the next, till my father held his head in his hands.

So one night I set myself on a stook and watched as the stars ran up the sky. Near midnight, such a hubbub came on, one would have thought the Judgment was at hand. Little Men covered one of the stooks, each grabbing a stalk and crying "Away! Away!" in voices no man ever used. And the stalks shivered, swelled, and sprouted into fine tawny horses. The Little Men jumped onto them and galloped out of sight, faster than any eye could follow.

When it was but a single stalk left, I jumped up to grab it, cried "Away! Away!" and galloped off. In less than no time, I was inside the mountains of the eastern world, in a deep and wonderful cave. The Fairy Queen herself sat at the head of a dining table that would have stretched from Donegal to Cork. We ate of everything good that the world can make, and of some things that the world cannot make, and when we finished there was such music as has never been heard or seen in this fair land. The Fairy Queen herself asked me to dance. "Never in life," I told her. "They'll be searching the world for me if the dawn finds my bed empty."

But the Queen would have none of that. "My dear, it's only one dance in a young night, and then you'll be home faster than you came." So I took the one dance, and afterward she brought me to a tawny horse.

"Promise you'll come again," she demanded as I climbed up. When I promised, she squealed in laughter and set the horse agalloping. We were home just at break of day, and when I leapt off, the horse shriveled to nothing but a barley stalk.

But it was to a strange place I'd come. My father's farm was gone, and a new house built in its place. Every hill, every stream around me was the same, but up and down the road there wasn't a house or hut that I knew. I called to a lad in the house, "Can you tell me of the home of Donal O'Sheary of Tawnawilly?"

He had never heard the name. "Could you ask of your

ma?" I said. He did, and she said again that no one in
Tawnawilly went by the name of Donal O'Sheary. But
when the grandmother, older than the hills, came out
she remembered the tale of a Donal O'Sheary who
disappeared with the Fairy Folk. No sign of him was
ever seen, and his father died of the grieving.

"I am Donal O'Sheary," I cried, "gone this long with
the Fairy Queen." But they would not believe it, so I
left Tawnawilly, carting my broken heart.

THE HOUSE HAD GROWN QUIET with Donal
O'Sheary's tale. Sorcha got up to stir the hearth-fire
embers, and when she set the poker down, Donal
O'Donnell could see tears scouring her cheeks.

"They say," said Donal O'Donnell quietly, "that in the dim world, there is more life and joy than ever in our own."

"Is it true," whispered Sorcha to the peddler, "that those who've gone on to the dim world, even the little ones, are happy, as you were there?"

"It may be so," said the peddler.

Donal O'Donnell stood and laid his hand on Sorcha's back. She held her face away from the firelight.

"So was it to the dim world that you went, then?" asked Donal O'Donnell.

"Only the Dear knows," said Donal O'Sheary, "but it's a wonder for all that."

"If it's wonders you'll be telling of," said the second peddler, "I've a wonder that will put haystacks and horses to shame."

Donal O'Donnell brought Sorcha's hand to his cheek. "Say it then," he said.

And so Donal O'Neary did, and he told this tale.

The Tale of Donal O'Neary

♦ THE SECOND PEDDLER ♦

By the white shore of Teelin stands the great well of the world, with the sweetest, coolest, clearest water in all Ireland. One summer's eve, my father sent me to fetch a drink after the threshing. But when I roped the buckets and looked deep into the well, what should I see in the water but a reflection of that white shore with a boat sailing by it. When I turned to look behind me, there was the boat, gliding on the sweetest wind.

"Donal," I said to myself, "leap into the boat, will you now, and see where it's to take you." So down I went, leaving the buckets by the well.

I sailed to the west—and me without a loaf of bread or a jug of sweet water! But I never felt hunger nor thirst, and never felt loneliness, even when the shore of Teelin sank beneath the waves. The sweet wind itself fed me until the evening of the third day, when the clouds pulled up a land as green as green. The boat glided to it and ran in on a shore as white as that of Teelin, and even whiter.

It would have been the world's pity never to have seen this place. Green meadows hunched up to higher hills, and the higher hills soared up to mountains, and from them fell the water in sheets as green as the meadows. Flowers as big as your hand filled the trees, and the birds that settled among them sang songs to pierce your heart.

Never in life had I thought to be so far from the shores of our farm. I spent the days splashing in streams, plucking ripe fruit, climbing gorges. At night I clambered into the trees and slept with the starry sky pulled over me. Not a chore beckoned. Not a cow to milk, a goat to pen, a stable to muck out. Always high summer it was and never winter. And all the time the sweet wind blowing.

But one day, I took a longing to put my hands to a rake, to smell the sweet grass heaped high in the barn loft, to smooth the silky snout of our old cow. I went down to the shore to see if I could glimpse the coast of Ireland, and there came the boat, gliding by as it had once before. I waded out to it and watched the waves sink the island.

Three fair days and three fair nights to my old home, until I saw the well I'd drawn from so long ago. I leapt to the shore for a drink. The buckets sat where I'd left

them, and when I dropped one down into the well, I saw in the reflection the boat asail. I turned. It was gone, and there was my own mother calling me to hurry on with the water, as if I had been only a moment away.

I dropped the other bucket into the well and took up the chores. And the sweet wind blew all the time.

"IT IS A WONDER that you say," said Donal O'Donnell, "that a boy should pass out of this life, and then come back, and none the wiser but himself."

"I'd travel a lee and a long road to shake the hand of any man who saw a greater wonder," said the second peddler.

"It's in the coming back that the wonder lies," whispered Sorcha.

"And if they cannot come," said the second peddler, "we bring them back in the tales we tell."

For the first time in who can tell how long, Donal O'Donnell and Sorcha looked fully into each other's eyes. "We bring them back in the tales we tell," repeated Donal O'Donnell.

"Oh, my dear," said Sorcha, so quietly that no one else heard but Donal O'Donnell.

Then the third peddler stood up. "A wonder it is that you say, Donal O'Neary," he said, "but I've a wonder to match."

"The Dear only knows if you've a wonder greater than that of Donal O'Neary," replied Donal O'Donnell, not taking his eyes from Sorcha. "But tell on."

And so Donal O'Leary did, and he told this tale.

The Tale of Donal O'Leary

◆ THE THIRD PEDDLER ◆

On a May day, when the Fairy Folk were abroad, my father set me turf-cutting on the bank of the River Strile, where peat is lovely, soft, and green. It was as hot a day as I could remember, and when noon came I'd have given my soul for a drink. And with the thought, a spring as clear as the bluest sky bubbled up at my feet.

I dropped to my knees, scooping up water. It was snow cold, and I shivered—for good reason. Though it was high spring when I knelt down, it was midwinter when I stood up, the snow and the wind blowing around me and the turf frozen under my feet.

Strange and very strange. But stranger still was what happened to me: I found myself the priest of a parish, doing the duties of a priest. I walked back from the bog into the parish town I had never seen before, but I knew every house as if I had been born there, and every soul that I met greeted me, and I blessed them as

I walked by. It seemed there was no wonder to me or to my people, for I knew them all as if I had been among them since the day I was weaned.

So for seven years my life was parish work, me a boy of no more than ten, now a priest of twoscore years. There was not a day without sickness to tend, new-borns to christen, couples to wed, old ones to bury. There was not a morning when I did not sing the holy service, and there was talk that it would be the bishop's chair that I sat in someday.

And it was to the bishop I was going, on a May morn, and traveling through the heart of a wood, when I came upon the loveliest spring, as clear as the blue sky and bubbling in the middle of the road. I knelt down and drank, and the water was snow cold. When I stood up, I was back on the bank of the River Strile. And there was never a spring to be seen, nor never has again in that part of the world.

When I reached home, my father's face opened. "My son, come alive again after so many years? Is it my son?" He ran his hands up and down me to see that I was solid and real, and told how the Dead Masses had been read for me.

While I told him all that had happened, he watched me as though I was like to disappear again, and often he reached out to touch me. When I went to sleep that night, he watched. And he was there in the morning when I woke, tears in his eyes.

I stayed in his house till he died, and there was not a night we did not tell that story again, of how the Fairy Folk took me away, and how glad we were that they should have brought me back."

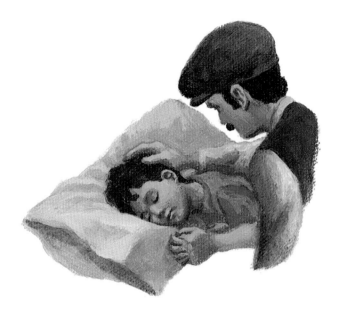

_ʘ⁄_ "IT IS THE GREATEST WONDER that ever you say," said Donal O'Donnell, "that a boy can be given up for dead, then found again. It is a wonderful happening, the most wonderful tale these ears have ever heard told."

Outside, the wind softened. Donal O'Donnell knocked his ashes into the peat and rose to unbar and unbolt the door. When he looked out, he saw the moon hooked into the sky, silvering Slieve Bernagh with its shimmering. Far away, the warm lights of Killaloe flickered.

Donal O'Donnell turned. "You'll be staying the night," he said to the three peddlers, "late as it is and darker than dark." Sorcha had already climbed to the loft to spread the bedclothes.

Donal O'Donnell and Sorcha

❦

So the peddlers stayed the night in the home of Donal O'Donnell. And while they slept, Donal O'Donnell and Sorcha sat hand in hand in the open doorway, looking into each other's eyes, warmer than the lights of Killaloe. The Dear knows how long it had been since they had sat so. They told stories to each other of their boyo—gone, but now somehow come back, and bringing green grass and bright air and cold water to their hearts. Their tears fell into their smiles, and all the while the sweet wind blew past them and filled the home of Donal O'Donnell and Sorcha.

Sure, that a story can unbar and unbolt a heart, that is the greatest wonder of them all.

AUTHOR'S NOTE

ANY STORYTELLER who tells folktales looks for ways to show how such old tales speak powerfully to new listeners. Sometimes stories can speak powerfully when they remind us of ourselves. Sometimes they speak powerfully when they tell us something about our own world. And sometimes they speak powerfully when several of them come together and, in coming together, show something that any one of them alone might not have shown.

And that is what I have tried to do here. *The Wonders of Donal O'Donnell* is really three stories wrapped within a fourth story. Usually the tale of Donal O'Donnell and Sorcha is a story about a struggle between a husband and wife. But it seemed to me that there was more than simply an argument that was going on in this story. And so into the middle of their struggle, I have placed the tales of the three peddlers, each of which is about a boyo who is lost and then found again—each time in a way more and more wonderful. They point out what neither Donal O'Donnell nor Sorcha will speak about: their own struggle with sorrow over the loss of their son.

Of course, the three peddlers are only telling stories to keep themselves out of the storm and close by the fire. To do this, they know they have to tell stories of great wonders. So they tell stories of the Fairy Folk, the mischievous creatures who live invisibly in the green hills and caves of Ireland. They remember stories of the great giant Finn M'Coul. And they make up fantastic places—Tawnawilly, the shore of Teelin, the River Strile—all in the hope that their stories will be so strange and so wonderful that Donal O'Donnell will not shush them out the door. (Not all of the places are made up, though. The village of Killaloe and the mountain Slieve Bernagh are both in County Limerick in south central Ireland, and when Donal O'Sheary tells of a table that would stretch from Donegal to Cork, he is telling of two real cities, Donegal being far in the north of Ireland, Cork far in the south. It would have been a mightily long table.)

Sure, Donal O'Donnell and Sorcha know that the peddlers' stories are too wonderful to be true, and yet, hearing tales about a boyo who is gone and then returned, brings to mind their own boyo. Now they see that barring and bolting the door against stories of him—even if it hurts to remember—means only that they forget him, and perhaps each other, but not their sorrow. And so the peddlers gain a night's lodging, and Donal O'Donnell and Sorcha find their boyo again in the stories they tell about him in the silver moonlight outside their opened door.